Unwired Love

A Gripping Story of Betrayal, Fear and Lies

L.M. NA

DEDICATION

To everyone who experienced hurt in a relationship and felt lost. Believe that there is good out there and that you deserve love and happiness. You are worthy!

CONTENTS

DEDICATION — i

CHAPTER ONE IS IT WORTH IT? — 1

The Genesis Of A Great Downfall — 4

CHAPTER TWO RED FLAGS — 8

Red Flags and The Girl That Couldn't See them — 11

Red Flag #1 — Fake House Fake Car — 11

Red Flag #2 — The Jobless Dad To Be — 12

Red Flag #3 — More lies and Getting Threatened — 14

Red Flag #4 — Getting the rug pulled underneath my feet — 16

Red Flag #5 — The Art of Being Used — 18

CHAPTER THREE NOT SO INNOCENT AFTER ALL — 20

I Was Gamed Hard — 21

The Most Expensive Prank Ever — 24

CHAPTER FOUR MAYBE MOVING IS THE CHARM — 27

The Plot of Hiring A Gorgeous Nanny — 29

Catching Him Red-Handed — 30

CHAPTER FIVE WHO IS THIS GIRL REALLY? — 34

A Lesson in Madness — 36

Making the Decision of My Life   39

Wrapping My Head Around it   42

CHAPTER SIX A NEW HOPE   43

Getting My Life Back On Track   44

Over to You   46

ABOUT AUTHOR   48

ACKNOWLEDGEMENTS   49

REFERENCES   50

CHAPTER ONE
IS IT WORTH IT?

"Love is totally nonsensical. But we have to keep doing it or else we're lost and love is dead, and humanity should just pack it in. Because love is the best thing we do."

Josh Radnor

Relationships are undeniably one of the highlights of our lives. We started building relationships from when we were little. Our relationships start at home with our parents and siblings, then we make friends at school, in the neighborhood, and in other areas as we grow up. But, everyone eventually reaches that stage that calls for a unique type of relationship — starting a new family and having wonderful kids.

Being a member of a loving family can be wonderful. Apart from the companionship that comes with a family, you get numerous advantages such as better finances, better taxes, less stress, a healthier lifestyle, and increased happiness and satisfaction.

You get to make plans with someone that loves you. A family can always do more together than the members can achieve separately. It's only sad that very few people ever get it right.

Love is that quagmire we all get lost in. The divorce rate per 1000 married women is now nearly double that of 1960. A couple completes a divorce every 13 seconds in America, according to reports from WF lawyers. If you don't know what that means: that's 277 divorces per hour, 6,646 divorces per day, 46,523 divorces per week, and 2,419,196 divorces per year. About 1500 divorces occur in the time it will take you to see a movie at the local theater.

Why does this happen?

This is the question numerous experts have been trying to answer for decades. If you have some hours to spend, you can find thousands of studies and statistics both online and offline about every possible factor that might affect marriages and lead to divorce. However, I'm not naive enough to claim that divorces are caused by a single factor.

Myriads of factors lead to divorce and it's different for everyone. You would agree that the foundation of a relationship matters. Far too often, we rush ahead into a relationship and marriage without considering everything we should. I have been a victim of this myself.

I once rushed into marriage and was blinded by my passion. It took reaching rock bottom for me to come to my senses. I may have seen the signs from the start of the relationship, but I chose to go ahead anyway.

Although love is often beautiful, you should know that not every relationship is meant to last. Not everyone is compatible with each other either, nor will some people ever be. Our greatest undoing is believing that our case may be special and failing to ask the tough questions. How often do you ask yourself the following questions?

- Is this worth it?

- Is my partner really worthy of me?

- Do they have the right traits and behaviors?

- Is it enough that they make me happy?

- Can I cope with their shortcomings for a year? Ten?

- Do I want my child to have this person as a parent?

Of course, I asked none of these questions and I don't think you do either. I think this is enough introduction, let's get started with my story.

The Genesis Of A Great Downfall

My love story commenced when I was a 27 years old single woman living in Los Angeles. I was the perfect social butterfly and I had a lot of friends, both close and casual. I had a decent life going on back then. Think of that typical social woman with a good career, who was financially stable and with her apartment. That was me. I was an entrepreneur with my own production company. In addition, I hustled on the side as a part-time freelance business consultant. I believe I had everything going well for me. The only thing missing was love and a family to call my own.

Considering my age, I decided that it was time to settle down since I had every other thing I wanted. Being a modern and socially independent woman, I wasn't comfortable with the conventional dating norms. I wasn't the kind of girl who dates guys who knew my friends. I didn't want to have my friends arrange dates or set up blind dates for me either.

Considering my options, I eventually concluded that online dating was the most viable option for me. And that was how I promptly signed up to Match.com and decided to try my luck. My target was any tall Asian dude, financially stable, and who has his ducks in a row.

I was ready to settle and I wanted someone who desired the same thing. That was my driving motivation. As fate would have it, it didn't take long before I started meeting people. It didn't take long either before I met the man who appeared to be the man of my dreams.

I had been chatting with some guys before Brian, but his profile was particularly interesting. We started chatting and soon got to know each other better. Within a short time, we clicked and decided to meet. We set up dinner and he was the perfect gentleman. He seems so normal and handsome and was so respectful that he opened up doors for me. He was too good to be true and he turned out not to be.

But, I couldn't resist his charms. He made me giddy and light on my feet like a little girl. I fell pitifully in love with his good manners, charms, and smile. We started dating afterward and it was fun and exhilarating at the same time. I was the cuddly girl newly in love once again. You've probably been in this situation too — meeting someone and being swept off your feet. There's absolutely nothing wrong with this.

The problem is that our heart can at times be the death of us. We follow the heart instead of trusting our brains.

I wish I could deny it but all signs were there. And although I was blinded by my passion, my friends weren't. I could remember what transpired the first day we had dinner with some of my friends. Out of the blue, one of my besties pulled me to the side and offered to take me on a getaway trip to China just to get me away from him. She told me she wasn't comfortable with Brian and I should stop seeing him if I could. "You don't know this guy," she said.

Ironically, she wasn't the only one to warn me. Everyone seemed to get bad vibes off of Brian and they kept warning me to thread safely. Of course, I didn't listen to them. I was blinded by love and my desire to have my own lovely family. I ignored logic and went fully with my heart. Since I knew he was attracted to me and I ignored everything everyone said. He was fine and I was fine, what could possibly go wrong?

At some point though, I did a little investigation about the bad vibes people got off him. I thought he probably had a nasty secret he was hiding from me. After about a month of going out together, I asked him if he had a secret he was keeping from me that I needed to know going on. I was expecting him to say "Yes," but that's exactly what he said.

He told me just got out of prison three months ago after serving a sentence of three years. He narrated how he came out in a pretty bad shape, with a broken rib, and how he was still in recovery when he met me. When I asked for the reason for his sentence, he said someone had mistakenly sold some stolen TV to him. On hearing that, I got empathetic because he appeared to be the victim and the news calmed me. I believed that it was a stroke of bad luck and it wasn't anything serious.

I believe you can see the red flags already. Going to prison isn't that big of a deal. However, he could have easily been fully honest with me from the start. I believe honesty is one of the core foundational elements of any successful relationship. Instead, he had chosen to wait until I came up with the question. As usual, I didn't think too much about it. Fast forward another month into the relationship and we decided to get engaged. Another red flag on my part.

This decision sealed my fate. This decision to get engaged led to my meeting with his parents and that was the icing on the cake. I met his adopted parents and they were the nicest and most adorable people on earth. There was only one word to describe them: Perfect. My mind was made up immediately after meeting with them. I had thought that since his parents were a nice Mormon family, he had to be a nice person, too right? I have never been so wrong.

It turned out I was wrong and you'll find out more about my story in the next chapter. My point here was that rushing into a relationship can be harmful. If you move slower in your love life and get to truly understand your partner, you can start seeing some signs. People can only pretend for so long. If you look hard enough, you will see the signs. You may end up recognizing that it's not worth it. You can later realize that you deserve better and that your partner can't offer you the peace and companion you wish for.

CHAPTER TWO
RED FLAGS

"To know when to go away and when to come closer is the key to any lasting relationship."

Doménico Cieri Estrada

Think of Antarctica for a moment. If you've ever been there or seen a picture, think of those huge icebergs taking up the horizon. They look enormous right? But what if I told you that what you see on the surface is only 1/10th of the actual ice. Icebergs have a slightly lower density than seawater and as such, only a fraction of the ice floats above the water.

By now, you are wondering what icebergs have in common with your relationships. What they have in common is that people can be masters of deception. Many people are more than they seem and are similar to icebergs to an extent. On meeting them, they win us over with their confident charms and wonderful behaviors.

Unknown to us, there is a lot brewing under the surface. Looking at this, it shouldn't surprise you that many marriages fail. Marriage is hard work.

Think about it, relationships are tasking and there's no easy way about it. Every couple are two different people with different personalities, habits, and temperaments trying to coexist in the same home.

Living together harmoniously doesn't always work out because falling in love isn't everything. Studies have proven that the euphoric feeling of love doesn't last. In time, it fades and both partners have to start caring intentionally about each other.

With that said, you can't expect mere feelings to keep a relationship going forever. At some point, you'll need to come together for some things and feelings just won't cut it. In time, you'll both need to plan about finances, family, work, and the likes.

You'll need to discuss who sorts out this bill or that bill and so on. In addition, you'll have to work things out about your work-life balance, family differences, how to raise your kids, where to live, and more.

Personality differences will set in at some point and that comes with its own range of issues. For instance, while a partner might prefer hanging the laundry, the other might prefer meticulous folding of the laundry. You might wish to park the car in a way that is different from your spouse. Your partner may be a fan of another football club or share a different ethnic or religious belief. These things might seem minor but they heavily impact a relationship.

Then there's the issue of loyalty and boundaries. Everyone has their own unique needs and boundaries in a marriage. Most people expect to be regarded highly by their significant other. Some people don't care, they give their partners more freedom to be themselves. Also, while your partner might be okay with you seeing someone when you're still dating, he or she may expect you to stop that after marriage.

Some partners require open feats of affections; they want surprises parties, flowers, and gifts. Some don't want you talking with members of the opposite sex anymore. Failure to meet these special needs often communicates that one partner doesn't care. If this goes on for long, resentment sets in.

But there's no relationship without these things. In fact, these aren't all the challenges present in relationships. So why do some relationships thrive when others don't? Well, there's no simple answer here. All I can say is that some things help. I believe traits such as communication, commitment, honesty, forgiveness, listening, and empathy help. As you can see, there's a lot that goes into making a happy couple. This is why screening one's partner is a must.

There's a need to look beyond all superficial sweetness and acts of affection. It's essential not to get carried away and see what's underneath the surface. Many sweet guys and gals out there are masters at deception. You have to look for red flags because people are only so good at hiding their dark side. Don't be scared to ask hard questions or do a little research.

A quick research on Google can save you from a nightmare down the line. Of course, I didn't do that. I did the exact opposite and I now hope you can learn from my story and maybe, just maybe you'll catch some red flags of your own.

Red Flags and The Girl That Couldn't See them

After meeting Brian's parents, I didn't slow down at all. Since my mind was made up and we were making progress in the relationship, we decided to get pregnant. He wasn't opposed to having a baby and he just agreed that we'll get married later on. This turned out to be the prelude to the first true red flag I should have seen.

Red Flag #1 — Fake House Fake Car

A month after we agreed to get pregnant and guess what? I did get pregnant. I was so elated and that was when I decided to move in with him. I thought it would be a good idea to move in together since my mortgage was double what he claimed to be paying for a mortgage. As an industrious woman, it seemed to be the only right move. He claimed to own the house he was living in and the car he always drove around.

Imagine my shock when I learned that none of this is true! After moving in, I got the shock of my life on learning that not only did he not own the house, he didn't own the car either. The owner of both the house and the car lived in the back of the house. There I was thinking he was only trying to impress me. I thought, "There is no problem about not owning a house yet, right?"

Mind you, I was pregnant at this time. Shouldn't he have been a little bit more honest? As you can see, the lies keep on building on each other. This is how we fool ourselves in relationships. We explain unexplainable things to ourselves. However, at times no matter how we interpret a red flag, it stays a red flag. Ironically, he was only getting started.

Red Flag #2 — The Jobless Dad To Be

Believe me, I'm not trying to sound like a downer, but you'll agree with me that raising a kid is expensive. There's a reason some people wait to be financially free before having kids.

When you're a parent, on top of your own personal bills, you get to spend on feeding a new baby, getting new sets of clothes, and paying for education and any health problems that come up. Couple this with the fact that you may have to work less to cater for the baby, while still paying more bills.

Now, who brings a kid to the world without any viable source of income? That would be my ex and I. After just one month of living with him, I realized that Brian has lied to me about working. He was in fact jobless and I also realized he was obsessed with gambling. But that wasn't the worst part of it.

If you talk with experts, they'll inform you that gambling is a brain disease. Every gambler believes that they'll always win and that one big win is enough to offset their losses. This pushes them to go to any lengths possible to get more money to keep gambling.

So maybe he couldn't help it. Maybe he could, I'll never know. I woke up one day to find that a camera given to me as a present was missing from where I kept it. Fast forward a few days, and my computer joined the list of lost items. More things went missing shortly afterward. This went on and when I couldn't have it anymore, I confronted him.

He immediately confessed and said he had to pawn off my belongings to clear his debts. This broke the floodgates and this was the first time he made me cry. I cried my eyes out because I couldn't believe I was going to end up with such a person. I went on match.com to find a financially stable and sweet handsome man. I couldn't believe I was set on the path to being the wife of a liar, gambler, and now, a thief.

After this incident, I took some time to go back to school to get my license for skincare so I could open up a spa once I had the baby. I knew he was jobless but I didn't want my kid to have jobless parents. As time went by and the wedding date came nearer, few things changed about him. He remained as jobless as ever. Everything I got saved up slowly dwindled due to the bills that needed to be paid. I even had to cough up the money for the wedding rings the day before the wedding. Everyone could see what a bad idea this marriage was going to be. Everyone but myself.

Red Flag #3 — More lies and Getting Threatened

For a while though, things looked promising before the wedding. All of a sudden, Brian developed the brilliant idea of reselling cars. He told me that this is a great opportunity for him to make money to raise our unborn child. The only stumbling blocks were the lack of a warehouse, and money to secure inventory set things up. He promptly asked for my help and I had no option but to lend him a huge chunk of my savings.

He had a good friend named Dave who was the initial partner of the business. I have met Dave several times when we started dating and I saw him as a genuinely cool guy. They partnered together and worked together on running the car business. Little did I know that this was the calm before the storm. Everything looked fine for like two months before the situation got funny.

For starters, Dave suddenly stopped coming around. When I asked my ex about it, he said it was because they no longer met eye to eye. I never found out what transpired between them. A few weeks after he broke off with Dave, he introduced me to a new partner: Andy. Andy is the owner of an auto repossession business and I was glad that my man finally partnered with someone who knew his zeroes. Andy was so nice and I became confident in the business. But then, all hell broke loose a few weeks after.

At this time, I was six months pregnant. I was at home when I heard someone banging at the door so hard. I immediately got scared and on getting to the door, it's Andy with a gun asking for my husband. He said, "where is he?" I told him I had no idea and that he had to relax. I invited him into the house and asked him what was wrong.

To my surprise, he informed me that my husband had stolen $4000 from him in a car repossession deal they did together. I was like, "No way!" I told him we had money and that it was probably a mistake on my husband's part.

I was like maybe he was busy with business or something and that's why he hasn't gotten through to him yet. I urged Andy to calm down and promised him that I'll get him his money and it was probably only a misunderstanding anyway.

If you think that it's not; you are right. It wasn't a misunderstanding. When my hubby came home, he played along with my theory and said he was busy and would sort it out with Andy later. I left the matter alone but things went south quickly a week later when we got death threats from Andy. It was at this point that my lovely husband confessed that he had lost the $4,000 once again to gambling. He explained that he did this to get more funds to purchase more cars for his business. Only it didn't work out as planned.

When I asked him to pay him from the money in the business, he told me everything was tied in the business. If only I had been more inquisitive, I would have known this is just a new lie in a long chain of lies. To save my hubby from imminent death, I had to make a deal with Andy. I had to give him some jewelry worth north of $4,000 to cover the bad debt. On giving him the jewelry Andy told me blatantly that my man was a very bad guy who didn't deserve me. But of course, I didn't listen.

That time I sincerely believed that was the end of it. But I should have known better after seeing who he replaced Andy with. Although he could choose anyone, he chose to partner with his old pal freshly out of prison. Is there any better idea than to run a car reselling business with an old pal from prison? Nothing could go wrong right? Oh! It did.

Red Flag #4 — Getting the rug pulled underneath my feet

The next red flag was the most painful and the signs bloomed a day before the wedding. At this, I was seven months pregnant, rounding up skincare school, and desperately hoping that there's something left in the car business. I asked him what was left of my $30,000 investment and he said barely $500. He had lost everything and most importantly, he was unapologetic about it. Now, be sincere with me. How would you feel losing thirty thousand of your life savings?

This was the threshold for me. I had reached my breaking point and I broke down in tears again. Think about it, who fails her unborn baby before he takes his first breath? I cried and cried. But then, I realized that I couldn't keep crying. I decided to pick myself up.

I decided that I wouldn't allow this to happen to my marriage. I decided to give my husband a little more funds (10,000) out of the wedding gift cash as a restart. I concluded that I would go ahead with the wedding but it didn't turn out the way I envisioned.

Just as we were getting ready to hit the reception on our wedding day, he decided that was the perfect time to hit an auction. Can you imagine being left standing on your wedding day? Crying and hoping that you haven't been abandoned? Well, I was and for a good two hours, my husband left me standing.

This was a wedding in which his parents, all his sisters, two brothers, and all my closest friends; even my ex-boyfriend who was one of my closest friends for over 8yrs was there. My mom, sister, and brother were all present too. I was humiliated since I thought he was having cold feet. Fortunately, he managed to arrive 30 minutes before the marriage was over.

As you can expect, I cried all through the entire occasion. I couldn't believe where I got it wrong. Everyone was scared for my marriage, even my maid of honor kept asking me if this was what I wanted. I of course brushed off all their concerns. Deep down, I loved my man and I believed I was making the right decision for my baby. I knew he loved me deep down or else he wouldn't be there marrying me on that day. If only I had known he had an ulterior motive for coming back.

Red Flag #5 — The Art of Being Used

To my surprise, his probationary office came airing the house a few days after the wedding. She said he was there to check up on him. Fast forward a few weeks later and he got a letter that his probationary period is over. To the government, he was now a model citizen. He was evidence that law enforcement works. From being a criminal, he was now an entrepreneur, with a beautiful wife and a baby in the works.

This got me thinking. What if what I misinterpreted as love wasn't love but a means to an end? Did he marry me to get out of probation? Then it clicked. I got to see all the red flags for the first time.

It didn't get better when I learned that he was once again out of money a few weeks after the wedding. He had blown the $10,000 on another bad decision. This time around, he has planned to open a legal cannabis company, whatever that means. But of course, he couldn't make it legal. His illegal business got raided by the authorities just after a few weeks and he was back to square one. Things were horrible to the extent that members of my family started blaming themselves for not objecting to the wedding.

This was when I thought for the first time: "Something has got to change!" I realized I needed a better atmosphere for my baby, far from away from where we currently lived. A month after my uneventful wedding, I graduated and passed my state board testing, I finally got my esthetician license. As luck would have it, my plans coincided with that of my elder sister. Just around that period, she planned to move permanently to San Diego. To get over the current issues, we planned to move in with my sister's home in San Diego after my baby is three months old.

CHAPTER THREE
NOT SO INNOCENT AFTER ALL

"Okay, life's a fact, people do fall in love, people do belong to each other, because that's the only chance anybody's got for real happiness."

George Peppard

Love can be beautiful, but it can also be nightmarish when you are with the wrong person, which happened to be my case. One of the major problems with relationships out there is infidelity. And one of the reasons why I was so smitten with Brian all through the crazy times, was that I've never caught a whiff that he wasn't loyal.

He had always played the loyal card. For this reason, he held a special place in my heart and I trusted him 100%. However, an act can only go so far. It didn't take long for this true color to show.

Little did I know that Brian was playing "the game" on me. You've probably heard about this. Several years back, pick-up artists popularised an idea called "the game" for seducing women. The game is a series of tactics and ploys used by men to trick women, win our hearts, and have their way with us. It goes against everything a relationship stands for. Usually, a relationship is meant to be based on honesty. It should be about a man approaching a woman honestly and getting to know her.

The game is the complete opposite of how normal relationships work. It involves employing tools of deception and lies to portray extreme masculinity. With the game, men act like someone else just to win ladies over. It turned out Brian was playing a long-term game on me. If you can remember, in the last chapter, I once considered if he had an ulterior motive for marrying me. Well, it turned out he did! And once he got what he wanted, he stopped being loyal.

I Was Gamed Hard

If someone ever told you that having a baby was easy, it's a big lie. Although it's wonderful being a mother, it's unbelievably hectic. When you couple this with a turbulent wedding and a lying husband, it was a lot on me. After moving to San Diego with my Big sister to get a breath of fresh air, I knew I couldn't rely on her to sort out my family bills. I got a job as an international skincare advisor at a beauty firm to pay the bills. At the same time, I was racking up the experience to open up my spa someday.

I did this for two months before the miracle occurred — Brian finally got a job. This time, it was a completely legal job. He has found employment as a business dental consultant in a top firm. Since he was now bringing in money, I left my job to have more time for my baby. Trials of motherhood right?

This patch of good luck continued for a while and within a few months, we had enough to move into our own little apartment. Little did I know I was moving into a house I would be staying alone in. As soon as we moved in, Brian began talking about quitting his job and starting his firm because he was now doing so great.

He proclaimed that one of his company's clients has offered to be his main client and pay him good money. I was of course happy to put the bad times behind me. This is a mistake I see more times than I can count, over the years.

Far too often, partners in a relationship move on from nasty experiences too soon. All because there's a little change in behavior and character, we are quick to forgive and it's a decision that often ends in tears. Now, don't get me wrong. I have nothing against practicing empathy and forgiveness.

My point is that if you're in a relationship with a partner and you've already noticed several bad qualities, there's a chance that there's more. At times, life would be so much better if we choose ourselves and we move on early, thereby protecting ourselves. That is something I failed to do by the way.

The following month I finally opened my own little spa. This period was probably the happiest I was in a long time. Things really looked up back then.

For a moment, it seemed that I now had a responsible husband, a cute baby of my own, and my dream spa. Because it was my first time starting a business and I had lost a lot to Brian, I started out really small. Nevertheless, I loved it because I have always wanted to own a spa. Everyone worked out too because I quickly got clients and I was suddenly a very busy small business owner.

During this period, I decided to hire a nanny to take care of the baby while I worked. A few weeks later I got some news that showed me signs of what was to come. I had a friend named Natalie who works at a massage spa place. We were casual friends and we saw each other often. She came to me one day saying my husband had visited her spa, called up the owner, and asked for her services specifically. At the time, I thought nothing of her job because I was familiar with spas.

I initially thought nothing of this. However, she explained that her spa wasn't an ordinary spa. Her spa happened to be one of those illegal spas involved in the adult business. I was shocked at this revelation. It's shocking news. It isn't every day that you hear that your husband intentionally went to get laid, with your friend. She was embarrassed too, but I guess she felt the need to inform me.

Since I didn't know what to do, I thanked her. And after getting home I told my husband. As you're probably thinking. He denied all of it. He agreed to have visited the spa, but he said it was a casual spa and he didn't specifically ask for Natalie.

Not knowing who to trust, I called up Natalie and asked why she was pulling a prank on me, but she denied it and said she would never lie to me. So we agreed to disagree on the matter. But, a couple of days later, she called back to inform me that her boss just got a blackmail letter from Brian.

Apparently, he had threatened to report the spa to the authorities if they couldn't keep his activities confidential and stop messing with my family. Her boss is now furious and she informed me she didn't want any more problems and that our friendship was at an end.

Now I want you to answer a question. "If you were in my case, what would you do?" This incident threw me into a low mood once again. But, girl! I wasn't ready for what came next. In the few weeks after my husband's infidelity incident, my life was turned completely upside down.

The Most Expensive Prank Ever

The internet is a pretty powerful tool and I think you'll agree with me. There are so many opportunities online and the possibilities are endless. I came to realize the internet can be just as harmful as it is helpful. And unless you've been at the receiving end, you won't know just how brutal it can be. My problems began with the random texts I started receiving. All of sudden, all sorts of random guys started sending dick pictures to my phone line.

The pictures were accompanied with messages saying they would love to come around and that they knew where I lived already. Naturally, my first reaction was irritation, but it transformed into anxiety when the texts didn't stop. I texted one guy back and he made me understand the depth of my problem.

Ironically, someone had deemed it fit to put up an ad for me on craigslist. Only that it wasn't the usual ad. The ad contained a picture of me and my kids with a tagline that read, "House mom needs sex because my husband is working all the time."

Oops!

Another question. *"If this happened to you, how would you feel?"* As for me, I was scared out of my mind. Come to think of it, I had a little boy with me and that was all my personal information out there. Anyone could see where I lived and who knows what they could do. I was confused about who could have done this to me. As a concerned mother, I told my husband about it and replied to all the texts that it's all a big mistake. I told them I was a victim of a nasty prank.

Brian was quick to inform me that Natalie and her boss were likely responsible. Believing him, I texted Natalie and warned her. But, after reporting the incident to the police, they said they couldn't do anything because it was all online. But things only got worse. A couple days later, I received another text saying "Tell your husband to stop messing with my business or else I'll send someone to rape you and your son." Once again, all the fingers were pointing to Natalie and her boss.

At this point, I was sick and tired of it. After talking with my husband, I decided that we would file a restraining order. I began the process of filing the order but the judge ended up declining it on account that my evidence wasn't solid enough. The number that had sent the text was an online number and it couldn't be traced to Natalie or her boss. After this, I knew going back to the spa was not possible. The address of the spa was in the ad and I've had guys checking in there too.

For the sake of my child's safety, I made the difficult decision to move the location of my spa. This wasn't an easy decision because I was just starting and moving was expensive. Fortunately, I had my younger brother around. He had broken off with his significant other at this time. So, he was there to keep me company and safe. Until now, I haven't found out who put up the ad on craigslist. But I think your guess is just as good as mine! The incidents that followed also gave me a hint about who the culprit was.

CHAPTER FOUR
MAYBE MOVING IS THE CHARM

"No woman could love a cheater and not pay the price for it"

Rose Wynters

Studies have shown that upwards of 40% of marriages are involved in infidelity. It's a big deal and there are many explanations people give for engaging in it. My point is that regardless of what the motivations are, you'll agree that cheating is wrong. Nothing makes cheating right. Unfaithfulness goes against everything a loving union stands for.

A marriage is a union of two people to form something greater. It involves choosing to go above feelings and personal ambitions. It's hard and the sad reality we live in is that people cheat, and they'll probably always do. Statistics have proven that people have myriads of reasons for cheating. A very common one is frustration. When a partner tries to solve problems several times to no avail, they may get tired and start to stray away.

The partner may have second thoughts about getting married or get jealous over attention given to babies or other people. Personal baggage such as neglect, abuse, mental illness addiction, or having a parent who cheated are risk factors for cheating. Lack of communication and respect are other common risk factors. When a couple can no longer find comfort in each other, one of them may look elsewhere. But, the biggest risk factor for cheating will always be incompatibility.

As I've been saying, relationships are tough and most couples are far from perfect. One thing that helps in steadying the ship is commitment, and the strongest commitment comes when couples are compatible. When both partners are dedicated towards each other and have complementary traits, they are at the strongest. Even if there's frustration or emotional baggage, they can always work things out. By communicating frequently and working together, couples can keep the love alive.

But when a couple marries for different reasons like Brian and I did, it's the recipe for disaster. For commitment to work, it has to be a two-way thing, but we never had that. A marriage is doomed to fail when the commitment is one-sided. I loved Brian but I doubt he ever loved me. He needed me at some point but that was it. I should have seen the betrayal coming from a mile away. I'm in no way saying that I was perfect, but I didn't have to be. Brian married me for different reasons and when he got what he wanted, I became surplus to his plans. He would inevitably look elsewhere for his needs. I should have known there's more to the lengthy stays he's been having away from his son and me.

The Plot of Hiring A Gorgeous Nanny

After the nasty incident in San Diego, we relocated to Temecula because it was close enough to my sister's and Los Angeles where Brian worked. By this time, I was nearly burned out and all I wanted was to focus more on my family and create a happier home for my child. But as I said, the marriage was a wrong plan from the start because Brian had other plans. He was hardly ever at home.

After two more months, I was replenished enough to start working again. Luckily, I got an offer as a part-time executive personal assistant after reaching out to a few people. But the part-time job turned out to be more than I bargained for.

Although it paid well, I got so busy I barely had any time for anything else. I could only day I was lucky to have my brother around since he helped in babysitting my son and taking care of the home. I only saw Brian once a week because he was traveling for work all the time or at least that's what he said.

A month into my new job and I suddenly got an email from a girl claiming to have received my "Ad" for a nanny from a friend. For the life of me, I couldn't remember putting out an ad for a nanny. But because I was so stressed out, I thought it might be a good idea. So, I told her to come over. My brother was the sole babysitter and it would be nice to have someone take off some of the load. I emailed her back and she said her name was Kaitlyn, 19 years old and with loads of experience tending to kids. I set up the interview at a time Brian would be back from travel.

On a fateful day, I was surprised to see Kaitlyn turn up in short skirts and thigh-high socks. I had her come 30 minutes before my husband came around to have a feel of her personality. As I wasn't one to judge a book by its cover, I let her in the house and introduced her to my son.

I asked her the typical questions and the interview went quite well. I also tested her ability by letting her into the playroom with my son and having them spend some time. I observed that she was really sweet and responsible enough to take care of a child.

After the interview, I talked over her appointment with my husband and he seems okay with her. So we decided that we'll bring her back as a nanny in the future for our date nights. Little did I know that Brian and Kaitlyn knew themselves and they planned out this little fiasco. Brian was the one who instructed her to email me right.

Catching Him Red-Handed

The following week, I asked Brian if we could go spend a mini weekend at Palm Springs where he works and to my surprise, he said YES. For a while now, we've been drifting apart because we rarely see eye to eye. So, I was super excited that we are going on a trip together as a couple. But as usual, things didn't exactly pan out the way I planned.

We planned to spend the weekend and go to dinner together. As a loving wife, I was elated to spend some quality time with my man. But the day we arrived, I saw some things that shook me to my core and it started with the simplest of things: shampoo. If you can believe it, I had forgotten my shampoo and conditioner at home.

When I told him, I was surprised when he told me nonchalantly to check for some under the sink. To my surprise, I did find some there and a bunch of other women's toiletries. Mind you, this was a man who has never shown a sign of infidelity to me. So I was more than shocked.

I was dumbfounded since I knew he never used any of the toiletries I saw. I approached him about it and that was when he lied. He told me nonchalantly that the owner sometimes lets out the rental when he isn't around. Now, let's think about this. We all know how rentals work. You pay for them and then it's yours alone until your rent is over. The only excuse that might have worked is Airbnb, but I guess he didn't know then.

Funny enough, I bought the lie as I was so in love with him and desperate to believe he is no longer a liar. However, the more time I spent at the rental, the more signs I saw that he wasn't being completely loyal to me.

When I was sweeping later that day, I saw there were lots of women's hair around the house and it wasn't my hair color. When I went to the patio, I also saw lipstick marks on the windows. However, every time I confronted him, he kept giving the excuse that it was the other people who rented the apartment. By now, you probably know that is not true.

What I have been seeing was evidence of his affair with someone else. Before we went out that night, he kissed me on the shoulder when I was getting ready. I guess he felt guilty because it's been a while since he's been affectionate towards me.

We went to dinner that evening, had a nice time, and had a quiet evening afterward. After we came back home, we made another plan to go to another dinner after a week. This time, I decided to call Kaitlyn to have her first nanny session.

On the way to the dinner, I couldn't help bringing up the topics once again. I told Brian I couldn't stop thinking about what I had seen at his place. I told him that we've been drifting apart lately and asked if he's been unfaithful because of all the things I saw in the house. If you can remember, he had the habit of confessing when I confronted him in the past.

Only now he wasn't so timid anymore, he suddenly became livid that I was even asking, and the conversation only heated up on our way to the dinner. At one point, I decided not to have his bullshit anymore and I told him I was going back home.

Only this time, I wasn't just going back home but I was leaving the house. I was a person who valued her mental health and needed some time to clear my head. I decided to go stay with a friend about two hours away, just to clear my head.

As I got home, I pleaded with Kaitlyn to drive me to my friend's since it was a bit late in the evening. I told her she could come back home if she didn't want to stay because I just wanted to leave. Little did I know that Kaitlyn, my remarkable nanny, was the owner of the hair strands I found at Brian's rental. Talk about living with the devil, right?

CHAPTER FIVE
WHO IS THIS GIRL REALLY?

"There is always some madness in love. But there is always some reason for madness."

Friedrich Nietzsche

Before we go on, I would like to discuss two more ideas about relationships in general. As I've mentioned earlier, a lot is required for a relationship to work. Romantic love doesn't last, a few years in and we all lose those giddy feelings and excitement.

At some point, you can no longer overlook character flaws because of love. The act of baby-making gets boring with time. And one day, you will wake up surprised that your partner is still there and you feel nothing. Differences will set in as time goes on and as I've said, these things are normal.

This is where open communication, loyalty, and commitment become important. I will now go further by telling you two more important factors: respect and trust.

Although everyone knows about respect, few people understand how critical it is to a lasting relationship. It's a trait you should always look out for in a potential partner. One thing you don't ever want to do is lose respect for your partner and it goes both ways. At times, this single factor can be more important than compatibility, communication, and even love.

At some point, communication will break down and all you'll have is respect. In my experience so far, I've learned that everyone fights. I've learned from studies that even successfully married 20+ year couples fight furiously. However, one thing these people retain is respect for one another.

Without the bedrock of respect, you will always question each other's intentions. You will judge your partner's judgment and feel the need to hide things from them. And this is when the cracks begin to appear. But it's not just about respecting your partner, you must respect yourself too. Self-respect is a sign of a healthy mind and it makes others respect you.

So, what do I mean by respect? Respect means not talking or complaining about your partner to others. Respect means trusting in their intelligence, creativity, and skills. Respect means accepting them as unique individuals with different perspectives. Most of all, respect means having no secrets.

Closely related to this is the topic of trust. Few things crash a marriage faster than holding secrets and not trusting your partner. This is why if something bothers you in your relationship, be willing to speak out. Doing this builds trust and intimacy. It may hurt in the short term, but that hurt is necessary because no one will fix your relationship for you.

With that said, trust goes deeper than the context of jealousy and infidelity. Trust is about believing that your partner has your best interest at heart. It's knowing if anything happens, you can count on them. It's about knowing they won't suddenly run away and start blaming you.

Sadly, few people look for these traits before settling down. Apart from the fact that Brian and I were practically incompatible, it was glaring that I never respected or trusted him. Looking back, it is also glaring that he didn't respect me. He never did anything to warrant my respect or trust, even though I did the best I could to win his trust.

A Lesson in Madness

One thing I still struggle to wrap my head around was why Brian brought Kaitlyn into our matrimonial home. It just shows how sick a human being can be. As you can see in my story so far, Brian did very little to warrant my trust, and it didn't get better after that night. On getting to my friend's house, as all women do, we got into a private discussion as I narrated my ordeal to her. I told her about how I never believed he was unfaithful but ended up seeing all those nasty things at his rental. I also lamented how I didn't know if he stays at his other rental in LA.

This was when the first bizarre thing happened with Kaitlyn. All of a sudden, she interjected into our conversation that she could locate his address. On enquiring further, she said we could find his address through the help of her friend who was a personal investigator. Looking back, this was the first mistake she made. Because after less than five minutes on the phone, her friend miraculously provided the address.

Think about it carefully. Even in the movies, it often takes the intelligence agencies like the CIA and FBI some time to locate the hideouts of people. Now, how on earth did a personal investigator find out the address of my husband in five minutes? On getting to the so-called address, we found a truck outside but nobody was home. So, Kaitlyn took us on a wild goose chase. Disappointed about getting the wrong address, we decided to head back home since it was getting late.

On getting home, I walked up to Brian and admitted that I was tired of all the lies. I made it clear that if I ever found out he was cheating, I would divorce him and not look back. As you guess already, at this point, I had very little respect for him. I had burnt through my reserve over the months. I still loved him to a fault but I couldn't bring myself to trust him.

The next few days zipped by quickly. Two days after our fight, he surprised me by getting me a vase full of wine bottles. He knew I liked drinking wine before bed so I appreciated the sweet gesture. I've since learned that bribing one's partner instead of making amends is a terrible habit. However, back then I thought it was nice of him.

The next day he had to travel back for work. Before leaving, he told me he had prepared coffee for me. Only that there was a nasty surprise to his early morning coffee. Initially, I had thought it was another delightful gesture but that was before I drank the coffee. It tasted as if the coffee had medicine in it. It was the worst coffee ever and I spat it out immediately. Ironically, that incident was another chunk of respect down the drain.

Can you ever trust or respect someone who tries to hurt you? I don't think I can.

Of course, he denied it when I asked him about it. "Maybe it was bad coffee," he said. But it turned out it wasn't just bad coffee because I collapsed the second day washing the dishes. I dropped to the floor clutching my chest and no one was home.

It took me minutes to eventually get up and contact the doctor for an appointment. Fortunately, the doctor couldn't find a reason for my sudden collapse. And that probably meant it had something to do with the coffee. But this isn't the striking event.

Right there at the doctor's office, I got a text saying "Your husband is having an affair." You can imagine my surprise. Funny enough, the message was sent by a number I didn't recognize and I got no response after dialing back. On confronting my hubby once more, he denied it blatantly and said it was probably a wrong number and a prank. But it wasn't. Because at 5 am the next morning, I got the text that brought everything into focus.

On waking up, I got the first text that read, "This is Kaitlyn's mom, your husband has been having an affair with my daughter." I immediately asked how she could be so sure, to which she replied, "We are a very wealthy family and my daughter doesn't have to babysit for money so I had her followed one day. She stayed at your husband's apartment overnight and I have photos of them kissing outside." This was when everything clicked, I could see the link between his extended stays away and the hair and lipstick marks on the patio, and the poisoned coffee.

Making the Decision of My Life

The only term that could describe my reaction is I blew up. After getting the text, I screamed at him historically, calling him all sorts of ungodly names. When I couldn't wrap my head around it any longer, I told him to leave and that I didn't want him anywhere near my son ever again.

Thankfully, he did leave without saying a word, which was heartbreak enough in itself. I went in to hug my child tightly and then told my brother what just happened. As you can imagine, he couldn't believe it and he asked what I was going to do. I decided enough was enough. I knew I deserved better and I decided to leave him permanently this time. Although for the short term, we would be staying with a friend of mine to avoid seeing Kaitlyn. I didn't want my child around such a psychotic human being.

This wasn't an easy decision for me and you would know if you have gone through a divorce before. The transition can be painful, but there was no going back for me. Over the weekend, Brian called to ask me if he could come to the house to get his things. I told him yes and that he could even spend the weekend enjoying the house for the last time. For the life of me, I didn't know he was going to take my word and act on it literally.

Before coming back home, I sought out a divorce lawyer and booked an appointment. On getting home, I was surprised to find my wedding ring missing from where I placed it. In addition, I noticed some truly weird things: my perfume was missing, there was female hair in the bathtub and my son's photo was also missing. I should say I was surprised but I wasn't. Talking to my brother, we figured out that Kaitlyn must have been in the house all through the weekend.

How? She had my keys from when she came to nanny!

Since Kaitlyn still had my keys for nannying, I had to call a locksmith to change the keys that day. I called Brian once more and warned him about his psycho girlfriend. I told him I was going to lock his girlfriend up for trespassing if I ever see her close to my house. He agreed that he would talk to her. I also informed him of my desire to move out of the house due to safety reasons. I also told him he would need to come to the house at the end of the week when I would have the divorce papers ready.

After five days the papers were ready, but he kept postponing our meeting until about 3 weeks later. Of course, I wasn't surprised anymore. He eventually signed an agreement that he could see his child during the weekend if he paid $3500 in monthly alimony. I moved out of the house and got a smaller home to start afresh.

But guess what? Brian never paid a single dime in alimony. I had to juggle three jobs: working as an executive assistant 5 day out of the week, a property manager part-time, and cleaning rental homes in my spare time. Once in a while, I took my family out for little getaways to clear our heads. But it was tough. Divorce is never easy regardless of the reason. I thought it would be easier after moving but the heartache didn't leave.

This heartache is the reason a lot of people run back to their partners. It is difficult to cope with, but I've learned that running back solves nothing. It's just setting up another disaster. I was glad I pulled through it. Things did get weird though. About a month after the divorce, I was stunned when Kaitlyn texted me saying she was pregnant from Brian. Only this time, things have gone sour between them. She was like I could keep him and she wanted nothing to do with him and she was aborting the baby. Of course, I told her never to contact me again and that she deserves what she's getting.

Wrapping My Head Around it

During a divorce, things get hard and you can start considering if you were the problem. Did you do something wrong? Is there a reason for their actions that you missed? As time went on, I was able to quench all these doubts. It was clear that day that he wasn't okay.

Brian's issues went far back to his home. He did a lot of things that eroded his parents' trust in him. All through the years, he has been lying and stealing from them. After the breakup, I got in a good relationship with his parents and they helped me cope with the transition.

Nine-month later, the divorce papers were finalized and I could breathe once more. I called his parents and thanked them for their support. I couldn't help but cry because my past was finally over. Now I was looking towards the future. I kept hoping that I would eventually meet someone out there who would love me for who I was and accept my son as his own.

CHAPTER SIX
A NEW HOPE

"To know when to go away and when to come closer is the key to any lasting relationship."

Doménico Cieri Estrada

A common divorce question out there is, "How long should you want?" This is a question without an easy answer. It's different for everyone so my advice is to do what works. For some people, it's a smooth transition as they are already seeing someone else. In my experience, I've learned this isn't the best question.

What we should be asking is, "Are you moving on the right way?" I've learned that it doesn't matter the length of time one takes. What matters is what you take away from the experience. At times as much as we like to blame our partners, we have some problems too. Nobody is perfect. And unless you fix your baggage, you'll only drag that baggage into the next relationship. There's no point playing the victim when there's an opportunity for growth.

After Brian, I thought a lot about my missteps and the little mistakes I had made. I realized I might have hurried too much and overlooked some things, these were faults on my part. I wasn't going to repeat this so I was reluctant at first to get into a new relationship.

One more thing I've learned about relationships is to control my expectations. I've come to realize that it takes two normal people to make a working relationship. So all I had to do was work on myself and find someone who was working on themselves too. Although I had my faults, it's undeniable that Brian wasn't totally okay. So moving on, I had to look for someone who was okay and I was ready to bid my time.

Getting My Life Back On Track

I would only be lying if I said I wasn't depressed after the divorce. I was. Big time even but I'm glad that my support network helped me all through or. I kept working all through it all. A few months after the divorce was finalized, my boss asked me to follow him to a convention in Las Vegas. He did this to get me out of my depression and I'm glad he did. I was still reluctant to go out and socialize but I later agreed to go. Little did I know that the trip would be one of the best things to happen.

On getting to Las Vegas, it was monotonous at first. During our second night, my job was to keep the company of my boss' friends and a girl he was interested in. We decided to kill time at the hotel center bar until the boss came back. I went scouting for a chair and by the time I came back, a random guy was talking with the girl my boss was interested in. Since it was my job to act in my boss' best interest, I went over to them with the intent of breaking it up.

I asked what his name was, and he told me, Lee. We shook hands and I immediately made it known to him that our discussion was over. But that wasn't the end of it. Turned out he had his eyes on me. Later on, he approached me once more when I went to the nearby slot machine to overcome my boredom. Lo and behold, he walked up to me and started engaging me in conversation. At first, I couldn't be bothered but since I wasn't busy I entertained his request.

He introduced himself and we made small talk. He asked what I was doing in Las Vegas, and I told him I was visiting with my boss. We also talked about our jobs, nationality and the likes and I realized he was interested in me. Mostly he was the one asking the questions and I was the anti-social girl. At some point, I wondered what the point of the conversation was since I probably won't be seeing him again.

Right after having that thought, I was surprised when he asked if I wouldn't mind hanging out later. I told him I had no problem with doing that since my boss was still around. On telling my boss, he was actually elated that I was getting out of my shell and asked me to invite him to the evening outing. At first, I didn't think he was going to show up, but he did after a while.

We all headed to the city and even ended up hitting a stripper club since one of us had to meet a friend there. At that point, I wondered what was going through Lee's mind and I was surprised to see he was still interested. When we later got down to sit and talk, I finally decided to take it seriously. But this time, I wouldn't be rushing and not asking the important question.

I asked him if he was married or divorced and if he had kids. I wouldn't be rushing into any relationship being ignorant anymore. It turned out that he just got divorced too. And the weird part was that his divorce was around the same time as mine, and so was the date of his divorce finalization. Lee had two girls, the same age as my son.

All in all, I was relieved to talk with Lee. It was soothing talking with him and I was back to that state of giddiness once again. We hit it off and the more we talked, the more it felt like I knew him even more. It was like the entire universe united to bring us together. We ended up spending the entire weekend hanging out and getting to know each other. But even though this had all the signs of a match made from Heaven, we agreed to bid our time. We would both learn from our past and make the best of our present.

Over to You

This is the end of my story and I hope you loved it. This also brings me to my last lesson: don't be scared of moving on. Earlier in this chapter, I mentioned that people have different time frames for moving on. The problem I've realized is that people often stay too long in their shells. Because of a traumatic relationship, they think everyone out there is bad. I don't hold this belief. There are both good and bad people out there and there will always be someone for you.

The most important aspect is learning from your past and improving your future. There are great people out there. It's all about having hope and taking your time in your relationship. It's about asking the right questions and making sure your relationships are based on the right principles. Always trust your worth and believe that someone great there is searching for you. You are worthy to find happiness and love. Thanks for reading my book!

ABOUT AUTHOR

L.M. Na, Lyne M. Na is a professional life coach, blog writer, entrepreneur, wife and mother of 4 who also writes children's books.

ACKNOWLEDGEMENTS

I would like to first thank my husband and soulmate for all the support and the endless asking "what do you think"? every time I finish writing something. thank you for your feedback, for nodding your head "yes, I like it", thank you for letting me write in the middle of the night in our bedroom while you try to sleep with my bright laptop or phone. Thank you for encouraging me to write again to spread my experience and inspire. to my boss, best friend, mentor Johnny; thank you for never giving up on me and always pushing me to do better, if it wasn't for you taking me to Las Vegas and telling me to follow my heart then this happy ending would never have been possible. a big thanks to my bestie Brandi for being with me during these past years and always having my back, without you I wouldn't know if I'd be standing right now. also, I would like to thank the universe for leading me to the path where I am now. But most of all I wanted to thank all my 4 children, without you I could've probably finished this book sooner. to everyone that knows I love them, you already know who you are so I won't mention a list of names. Thank you all for the love and support that you all gave me during this time of writing my first non-fiction book. But last but least, thank you to those of you that are reading this.

REFERENCES

Kelsey Hurwitz, (2021). 71 Relationship Quotes That'll Give You All of the Warm Fuzzies. Web. Accessed via https://www.womansday.com/relationships/g20888175/relationship-quotes/ Retrieved 10 October 2021.

Wong DW, Hall KR, Justice CA, Wong L (2014). Counseling Individuals Through the Lifespan. Sage Publications. p. 326. ISBN 978-1483322032. Intimacy: As an intimate relationship is an interpersonal relationship that involves physical or emotional intimacy. Physical intimacy is characterized by romantic or passionate attachment or sexual activity. Retrieved 10 October 2021.

Ribbens JM, Doolittle M, Sclater SD (2012). Understanding Family Meanings: A Reflective Text. Policy Press. pp. 267–268. ISBN 978-1447301127. Retrieved 11 October 2021.

Miller, Rowland & Perlman, Daniel (2008). Intimate Relationships (5th ed.). McGraw-Hill. ISBN 978-0073370187

Perlman, D. (2007). The best of times, the worst of times: The place of close relationships in psychology and our daily lives. Canadian Psychology, 48, 7–18.

Derlega VJ (2013). Communication, Intimacy, and Close Relationships. Elsevier. p. 13. ISBN 978-1483260426. Retrieved 11 October 2021.

Mashek DJ, Aron A (2004). Handbook of Closeness and Intimacy. Psychology Press. pp. 1–6. ISBN 978-1135632403.

Staff members, 2018. Wilkinson and Finkbeiner Family Law Attorneys. Web. Accessed via https://www.wf-lawyers.com/divorce-statistics-and-facts/

Mark Manson, 2019. "1500 people gave all the relationship advice you'll ever need." Web. MarkManson.net Retrieved 12 October 2021.

"Definition of LOVE". Definition of Love by Merriam-Webster. 27 December 1987. Retrieved 30 October 2021.

Roget's Thesaurus (1998) p. 592 and p. 639 Retrieved 20 October 2021.

"Love – Definition of love by Merriam-Webster". merriam-webster.com. Archived from the original on 12 January 2012. Retrieved 20 October 2021.

Fromm, Erich; The Art of Loving, Harper Perennial (1956), Original English Version, ISBN 978-0-06-095828-2 Retrieved 17 October 2021.

"Article On Love". Archived from the original on 30 May 2012. Retrieved 28 October 2021.

Helen Fisher. Why We Love: the nature and chemistry of romantic love. 2004.

"What Is Love? A Philosophy of Life". HuffPost. 5 December 2014. Retrieved 2 October 2021.

Liddell and Scott: φιλία Archived 3 January 2017 at the Wayback Machine

Mascaró, Juan (2003). The Bhagavad Gita. Penguin Classics. Penguin. ISBN 978-0-14-044918-1. (J. Mascaró, translator Retrieved 23 October 2021.

www.ingramcontent.com/pod-product-compliance
Lightning Source LLC
Chambersburg PA
CBHW070252310726
48976CB00008B/2635